Dear mouse friends,
Welcome to the world of

Geronimo Stilton

THE RODENT'S GAZETTE
EDITORIAL STAFF

 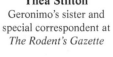

Geronimo Stilton
A learned and brainy
mouse; editor of
The Rodent's Gazette

Thea Stilton
Geronimo's sister and
special correspondent at
The Rodent's Gazette

 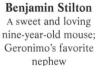

Trap Stilton
An awful joker;
Geronimo's cousin and
owner of the store
Cheap Junk for Less

Benjamin Stilton
A sweet and loving
nine-year-old mouse;
Geronimo's favorite
nephew

Geronimo Stilton

THE GOLDEN STATUE PLOT

Scholastic Inc.

ISBN 978-0-545-55629-3

Copyright © 2009 by Edizioni Piemme S.p.A., Corso Como 15, 20154 Milan, Italy.

International Rights © Atlantyca S.p.A.

English translation © 2013 by Atlantyca S.p.A.

GERONIMO STILTON names, characters, and related indicia are copyright, trademark, and exclusive license of Atlantyca S.p.A. All rights reserved. The moral right of the author has been asserted.

Based on an original idea by Elisabetta Dami.

www.geronimostilton.com

Published by Scholastic Inc., 557 Broadway, New York, NY 10012. SCHOLASTIC and associated logos are trademarks and/or registered trademarks of Scholastic Inc.

Stilton is the name of a famous English cheese. It is a registered trademark of the Stilton Cheese Makers' Association. For more information, go to www.stiltoncheese.com.

Text by Geronimo Stilton
Original title *Attacco alla statua d'oro!*
Cover by Flavio Ferron
Illustrations by Danilo Loizedda, Roberta Pierpaoli, Luca Usai, and Giuseppe Facciotto (pencils and inks); Giorgia Arena, Maria Laura Bellocco, Andres Mossa, Edwyn Nori, Nicola Pasquetto, and Daniele Verzini (color)
Graphics by Paola Cantone with Michela Battaglin

Special thanks to Kathryn Cristaldi
Translated by Julia Heim
Interior design by Kay Petronio

12 11 10 9 8 7 6 5 4 3 2   13 14 15 16 17 18/0

Printed in the U.S.A.   40
First printing, October 2013

A PERFECT TAN!

It was Monday morning, and I went to work wearing movie-star sunglasses and a perfect tan. Well, um, an almost-perfect tan . . .

I said hello to everyone and **RUSHED** to my office.

Oh, I'm sorry, let me introduce myself! My name is Stilton, *Geronimo Stilton.*

I run *The Rodent's Gazette*, the most

famouse newspaper on Mouse Island.

Anyway, where was I again? Oh yes. As I scampered by my staff, I heard them all whispering.

"Love the GLASSES!"

"So COOL!"

I closed the door to my office behind me with a SIGH of relief. Then I turned on all the lights and began to work, without taking off my sunglasses.

Okay, I know you're wondering why I was acting like some sort of famous celebrity. Well, I'll tell you. . . .

It happened that weekend when I went to the beach. I fell asleep in the sun for hours and hours. Too bad I forgot to take off my sunglasses. When I woke up, I was left with ridiculous white marks around my eyes! I looked like a reverse PANDA!

I was so EMBARRASSED, I decided there was only one thing for me to do. I had to keep my sunglasses on . . . at all times! I wore them at the supermarket, I wore them on the SUBWAY, and I wore them to work.

Of course, in order to read anything in my office I had to turn all the LIGHTS on, even though it was the middle of the day. What a waste of energy! I felt terrible!

The next morning I felt even worse. When I went to the office, my whole staff was wearing SUNGLASSES, just like me.

And they had also turned all the lights on, even though it was sunny! **HOLEY CHEESE!** I had started a trend! A trend of wasting **energy**!

Plus, I felt like I was working with a bunch of **SECRET AGENTS** (like my friend **OOK**).

I should have spoken up,

but I was still too embarrassed. *Things will get back to normal sooner or later, right?* I thought. Wrong! Instead, things began to spiral out of control!

A few days later, my CRAZY trend was spreading like soft cheese on a cracker. Soon all the mice in the city were wearing dark sunglasses. They wore them in their homes, on the street, everywhere. And they kept the lights BLAZING day and night.

Before long, so much electricity was being used in New Mouse City that there was a total BLACKOUT. Everything electrical shut down.

Since I couldn't work, I decided to take a walk by the water to think. As I stared out at the Mouse Island STATUE OF LIBERTY (also known by many as Mousey Liberty), I thought about what the statue stood for: freedom.

Yes, **FreeDOM** to be your own mouse.

I looked at my REFLECTION in the water. Then I took off my sunglasses and put them in my pocket. It was time to let everyone see the **REAL ME**: wacky suntan and all!

I was glad I could go back to being myself, but I still felt awful about wasting so much **electricity**. Suddenly, I was hit with an idea. I could write a book about the importance of saving energy!

But before I tell you that story, I want to tell you another one. This one is about electricity, too, and it takes place on (gulp!) **Cat Island**!

It all started when **Catardone III of Catatonia**, the king of the pirate cats, discovered they were having electrical energy problems, too. But let me start at the beginning. . . .

WHO TURNED OUT THE LIGHTS?

It was a quiet, peaceful evening at FORT FELINE on Cat Island.

OSCAR WILDWHISKERS, the pirate publisher of *The Cat Island Courier*, the most famouse newspaper on Cat Island, was relaxing in his tower.

He put on his soft mouse-fur slippers and sank into his favorite pawchair with his book *Catnip Soup for the Pirate's Soul*. Then he turned on some soothing music and sighed. Ah, what a *purrfect* life!

But then the lights went out and the music stopped.

"**Frozen fish fritters!** What's going on?" Oscar yowled. "This is the third time today that the power has gone down!"

ITCHY, Oscar's faithful butler, came rushing in. "I can't figure out what's wrong, sir. The electrical system seems fine," he reported.

Furious, Oscar closed his book.

"Get me the phone, Itchy!" he hissed. "I need to call my cousin **Catardone**. I don't know how that cat got to be **KING OF THE PIRATE CATS**. He's not exactly the

smartest cat in the alley, you know."

The butler **coughed**. "Um, sir, the phone doesn't work, either," he replied.

WASTE! WASTE! WASTE!

"**MEEEOOOW!**" Oscar shrieked. Then he got dressed and stomped down to Catardone's quarters.

The entire fort was completely **DARK**.

"What a disaster!" Oscar said to himself. "Without electricity, I can't turn on the copiers to print my newspaper."

Suddenly, a furious **YOWL** rang out from the Great Council Chamber.

"*FESTERING FLEA BITES!* I've had it!"

It was Catardone, the king of the pirate cats.

He had called together all of his feline advisors and the scientists who worked at the Catlab.

CATARDONE III
King of the
Pirate Cats

"Something needs to be done about this energy situation. WASTE, WASTE, WASTE!" he shrieked. "Would it kill anyone to remember to turn off the lights or the CLAW SHARPENER once in a while? We are going broke trying to pay the electric and gas company. The amount of money left in the IMPERIAL VAULT couldn't even pay for a quarter of a fish sandwich!"

Just then, Catardone spotted Oscar in the corner of the room.

"And you, Cousin!" the king continued. "Those printers for your newspaper are going NONSTOP!"

"Yes, well . . ." Oscar started to protest,

even though he knew it was no use. His cousin had always hated the paper.

Before Oscar could go on, a **slim**, young female cat strode into the room. It was **TERSILLA**, Catardone's spoiled teenage daughter.

"Daddy! Who turned off the electricity? I desperately need to **DeeP-CONDition** my fur and I'll need the electric fur-dryer when I'm done! What's going on?"

TERSILLA

14

THERE GOES MOVIE NIGHT

"I'll tell you what's going on!" Catardone **hissed**. "Everyone has been wasting so much electricity and fuel around here that we have run out of MONEY to pay our bills! So until one of you figures out a way to get us some GOLD, I've taken matters into my own paws and turned off the power!"

Gasps and sad meowing rose from the crowd.

"Oh, don't be such a bunch of kittens!" Catardone scolded. "We can use candles instead of lightbulbs, and instead of driving everywhere, we can walk. It's great exercise." Then the king added under his breath, "Though, of course, I will be pushed in the

ROYAL CARRiAGE, because I'm already in great shape."

Then he stood up, tripped over his own tail, and TUMBLED down the stairs. BONZO FeLiX and Boots, his trusty assistants, rushed to help him.

At that moment, one of the scientists from

the Catlab stood up. It was Dr. Regina Redfur.

"Your Excellency, I hate to complain, but you turned off the **electricity** just as we were purrfecting a new anti-flea portable shower system...." she began.

DR. REGINA REDFUR

"Oh yeah? Well, try getting **stuck** in an elevator for an hour!" interrupted Simon Scarsnout.

"At least your **FAVORITE** scallop-flavored ice cream didn't **melt** in your freezer!" Tomcat Pat whined.

"Who cares about ice cream?" Hillary Hotpaws

snorted. "I was in the middle of baking a gourmet **CATNIP** casserole!"

"Enough!" Catardone shrieked. "I can't take any more of this whining! I don't care about your shower system, your elevator, or your melted ice cream! I just told you, we've got to figure out a way to pay our energy bills, or invent some other way to make electricity. Until then, I'm keeping you in the D A R K !"

"There goes movie night," Tomcat Pat sniffled.

But Catardone wasn't listening. He had sidled up to Hillary Hotpaws. "Maybe you could make that catnip casserole over an open FIRE," he suggested. Just the thought of some tasty catnip had the king drooling like a rabid stray cat.

READY OR NOT!

Catardone was still dreaming of catnip when all of a sudden a tiny torpedo came **whirling** into the room and slammed into his ROUND belly. The king crashed to the ground in a terrified heap.

"HELP! Assassination attempt! Guards, save me!" he cried.

But when he looked up, he realized the torpedo was none other than his youngest daughter Kitty, who was ZIPPING around the room on her in-line skates.

"Kitty! What are you doing here? It is **WAY** past

BOING

your bedtime! Plus, I'm in the middle of a meeting!" the king scolded.

Kitty grinned, ducking behind her father. "Sorry, Pops," she squeaked. "But we're playing **hide-and-seek**, and **SCOUT** is just around the corner!"

Just then, a second kitten came CAREENING into the room on a **BLUE** skateboard. It was Scout, Kitty's twin brother.

"Ready or not!" the kitten cried, heading straight for Catardone.

A second later, he slammed into the king's belly, bouncing off it with a loud *boing*!

Once again, Catardone crashed to the floor. By this time, the king's advisors were all YOWLING with laughter. After all, it wasn't every day that the pirate cats got to see the king being made a fool of by two excitable little kittens!

Catardone was fuming.

NO PHONE?

Catardone stood up, trying unsuccessfully to fix his frazzled whiskers. Then he glared at his advisors, who grew silent. "You think this is funny?!" he shouted, accidentally poking himself in the eye with his hook paw. Everyone tried not to laugh.

Meanwhile, Oscar pulled Kitty and Scout aside to tell them about the ENERGY problem.

"Well, if we don't use a lot of electricity and gas, then we will not have as much POLLUTION," said Kitty helpfully.

Tersilla rolled her eyes. "Who cares about pollution?" she snorted, patting her head. "I'm having an important fur crisis here."

"I'm not worried about the fur dryer, but

without gas we can't use the **speedboat**," Oscar said. He thought for a moment. "Or the **CATGLIDER**!" he added.

"Even worse, without electricity we can't use our **computers** or charge our phones," Scout added.

Tersilla's eyes grew **wide**. "No phone?" She gulped.

"No phones," Kitty repeated. "So you can't call or text any of your friends."

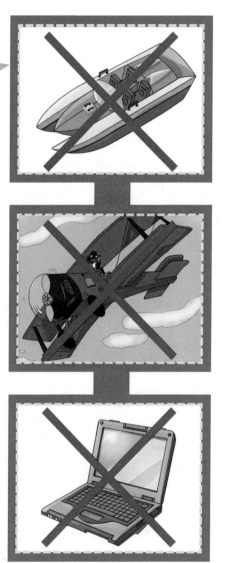

A GOLDEN STATUE

"What a tragedy!" Tersilla **MEOWED**. "Daddy! You've got to do something! I'm a teenager! I can't live without my phone!"

Soon, everyone was whining again.

Catardone clapped his paws for attention.

"Silence!" he ordered. Then he looked around the room.

"I didn't bring all you scientists here just to gripe. I brought you all here so you'd get your **TAILS** in gear and find a solution to our problem. So stop meowing and start moving!"

The scientists looked at one another blankly. No one had any brilliant ideas.

But just then, Dr. Redfur **MEOWED** excitedly. She turned to Catardone.

"I've got it, Your Excellency, Your Furryness, Your Hefty Highness — I mean, Catardone," she announced.

The king narrowed his eyes as the cat began digging through her bag.

First, she pulled out a pair of PAJAMAS, then a bathrobe, a toothbrush, some toothpaste, a brush, fluffy socks, and a bar of soap from her bag.

"I never know how long these URGENT meetings are going to last," she explained matter-of-factly.

Finally, she found what she was looking for. It was a map of MOUSE ISLAND!

"Here is the solution!" Dr. Redfur exclaimed.

The rest of the cats stared at the map, confused.

"Uh, what are we going to do with a map, Dr. Redfur?" asked Bonzo.

"Are we going to **BURN** it and use it as fuel?" asked Boots, scratching his head.

Dr. Redfur laughed. "Don't be an alley cat," she chided. She pointed a claw at the port of **NEW MOUSE CITY**.

"You see this?" she asked.

"Yes, it's **Mousey Liberty**," responded Kitty.

"Exactly!" said Dr. Redfur. "According to my scientific calculations, it is the only treasure that we should be able to reach without the use of a high-powered boat. We can take *The Black Hurricane*. All we have to do is get to the island and **STEAL** the statue."

"And we'd want to **STEAL** an old statue because . . ." Bonzo murmured, bewildered.

"Because . . . that old statue is made of

NEW
MOUSE
CITY

THE BLACK
HURRICANE

MOUSEY
LIBERTY

THE PORT

GOLD!" Dr. Redfur finished, smiling proudly.

At the mention of gold, Tersilla's ears perked up. She loved gold almost as much as she loved **tuna fish**!

Then Oscar asked, "But are you sure the statue is made of gold?"

Dr. Redfur's fur ruffled. "What kind of question is that? Of course I am sure the statue is made of gold! We are scientists

Scientific proof?

and, therefore, we have scientific proof. The statue is YELLOW, right? And gold is YELLOW, isn't it? So the statue is made of gold!" she insisted.

Oscar and the twins stared at Dr. Redfur skeptically. What kind of scientific proof was that? What happened to research? What happened to evidence?

But the king had heard enough.

"Of course! That makes **purrfect** sense to me! If the statue is YELLOW, it is obviously gold!" Catardone agreed. Then he hissed to get everyone's attention.

"Listen up, everyone. Tomorrow we will meet in a top secret location to prepare for our trip to NEW MOUSE CITY," he declared.

STATUES OF LIBERTY

IN NEW YORK . . .

The Statue of Liberty is located in the United States of America, in New York, very close to the island of Manhattan. It is a gift that the French gave to the United States in 1886, to celebrate the hundredth anniversary of American independence.

. . . IN PARIS . . .

To celebrate the hundredth anniversary of the French Revolution in 1889, the United States gave a gift to France: a bronze copy of the original statue. This statue is in Paris. It is only 37 feet tall, while the original is 151 feet tall.

. . . AND IN NEW MOUSE CITY!

The New Mouse City Statue of Liberty (also known as Mousey Liberty) was constructed after the Great War of Rats and Cats. The statue holds a piece of cheese in one paw, and, in the other, a book with the words of the New Mouse City anthem written on it. The seven points on its crown symbolize freedom.

THE P-P-PASSWORD?

The next day, Catardone, Bonzo, Boots, Tersilla, and the rest of the king's advisors headed to the secret meeting place in the underground offices of **The Cat Island Most Wanted Headquarters**. It's a place where they study all the ways to catch mice like (gulp!) me, *Geronimo Stilton*!

"Remember, this mission needs to be top secret," Catardone reminded everyone as they reached the soundproof office door.

But before they could put in the password, a cat in slippers and a robe came shuffling out, complaining, "This place stinks! The water in the shower is ice-cold!"

The king arched his back. "What is the meaning of this?! What is this stray doing in our secret headquarters?!" he shrieked.

Boots **CHEWED** his pawnail. "Um, it's nothing to worry about, Your Felineness," he soothed. "I thought it would be a good idea to rent out the space. You said we are **LOW** on cash."

"You mean **anyone** can come stay here?" Catardone demanded.

"No, of course not, not anyone," Boots explained. "I mean, they need to pay up first. And then I give them the **PASSWORD**."

The king gasped. "The p-p-password?" he

The water in the shower is ice-cold!

mumbled. Then he **fainted**.

Two hours later, the king woke up. By then his advisors had already organized the plan to sail to New Mouse City and steal the GOLDEN statue.

Later that day, Catardone laid out the plan to his crew. First they would prepare the king's ship, *The Black Hurricane*, for the voyage. Then, once they arrived at the port of New Mouse City, they would **knock** the statue down with cannonballs. Then they would tie it to the ship and **DRAG** it back to Fort Feline.

"It's a purrfect plan! We sail at dawn!" the king announced.

The Pirates cats' Plan

IT'S A PURRFECT PLAN!

1 WE LEAVE!

2 WE FIRE!

3 WE STEAL!

LET'S SAVE THE
OCEAN FLOOR!

Meanwhile, **scout**, *Kitty*, and **OSCAR** had listened to Catardone's plan also, thanks to a two-way radio hidden in the Most Wanted Headquarters.

What a strange plan!

"What a strange plan," remarked Oscar.

"It's not just **strange**, Uncle, it's fur-raising. Dragging the statue through the **SEA** will damage the ocean floor and hurt a lot of animals!" Kitty wailed.

"We've got to tell *Geronimo Stilton*," Scout said. "But how do we reach him?"

I wish I could say the cats decided to send me a Cheese-O-Gram, but they didn't. Too bad. I just love Cheese-O-Grams. You get a big basket filled with different types of cheese, and then your message is spelled out with **chocolate** cheesy chews. Yum!

But where was I? Oh yes. Just then, Oscar had an idea. You see, Oscar's eldest daughter, Samantha, loved reading my books. In fact, she even traveled to **Niagara Falls**, a place I described in one of my bestsellers.*

* Check out my adventure *Field Trip to Niagara Falls*!

THE OCEAN FLOOR
A TREASURE WORTH SAVING

The **ocean floor** is host to hugely diverse, unique species of animals and vegetation. Forests of algae and coral are found there, as well crustaceans, fish, and microscopic forms of all kinds. Parts of the ocean floor that are **rocky** host many types of fish, urchins, starfish, mussels, oysters, crabs, and lobsters. Parts that are **sandy** are the preferred habitat for sole, rays, sea horses, octopi, and shrimp. Some types of fishing, like trawling, put the plants and animals that live on the ocean floor in serious danger. The fishing nets are dragged on the floor and destroy the flora and fauna of the ocean.

MID-ATLANTIC RIDGE

EUROPE

AFRICA

SOUTH AMERICA

Did you know that ...

the longest mountain chain in the world is underwater? It is called the **Mid-Atlantic Ridge**, *and it extends from the Antarctic Ocean through the Atlantic Ocean (practically from one end of the Earth to the other!). Its length is four times greater than the Himalayas, the Rocky Mountains, and the Andes Mountains put together!*

"I know Sammy communicates with that literary rat all the time," Oscar explained. "She sends **messages** to him using a carrier pigeon. And I know just where to find the old bird."

"Great idea, Uncle!" the kittens MEOWED happily.

THUGSY AND KILLER

The next morning, as the carrier pigeon flew toward NEW MOUSE CITY with a message to me, the pirate cats prepared to board *The Black Hurricane*.

Catardone was already on the boat, **relaxing** in his royal suite.

At the top of the **GANGPLANK**, Bonzo recited the names of those who were to participate in the mission in a **solemn** tone.

" . . . Dr. Regina Redfur, Simon Scarsnout, and Princess Tersilla . . ."

Just then, **TERSILLA** stormed onto the gangplank, waving a paper in her paw.

"Bonzo, wake up! Didn't you get the new order?" she asked, SMACKING him in the snout with a piece of paper.

"No, the king didn't say anything —" Bonzo began.

Tersilla interrupted him. "Don't worry about the king. Dad is watching his favorite TV show, *Mouse Hunters*. You don't want to disturb him — you know how he gets," she warned.

Bonzo **shivered**. If there was one thing he knew about Catardone, it was never to bother him when he was watching

one of his shows unless you wanted your fur
REARRANGED!

"Okay," said Bonzo, taking the paper from
Tersilla. "Ahem, it says here that THUGSY
and KILLER will round out our crew,"
he read. "Hmm, I've never heard of them
before."

Tersilla led the two cats on board. "I'll
show them the ropes," she said, **pushing**
past Bonzo.

Bonzo wasn't sure what to make of the **new cats**, but he didn't have time to think about it. It was time to set **SAIL**. Bonzo got to work immediately.

In fact, he was so busy helping the crew, he didn't notice two other **furry** figures **CREEPING** up the gangplank. . . .

LOOK, A BIRD!

Back on Mouse Island, I was having a nice peaceful morning at the office of *The Rodent's Gazette*.

The electricity had finally turned back on, and I was showing the proofs of my new book on saving **energy** to my nephew Benjamin and his friend Bugsy Wugsy.

"Look, a bird!" shrieked Bugsy.

"He's a *carrier pigeon*!" observed Benjamin. "He's got a message tied to his leg!"

The pigeon began to **ZIGZAG** all over the room.

So much for a **peaceful** day at the office!

"I'll handle this, Uncle G!" Bugsy cried,

jumping onto my desk. A second later, she launched herself at the pigeon.

But instead of catching him, she knocked over the bust of Grandfather Shortpaws.

"NOOOOOOOOOOO!"

I yelled, diving for the statue. Grandfather Shortpaws never would have forgiven me if it had broken!

To my surprise, I caught it just in the nick of time. Why was I surprised? Well, let's just say I'm not very ATHLETIC. No one would call me a sportsmouse!

Anyway, where was I? Oh yes, I was watching the pigeon CIRCLING over my head when something occurred to me.

"I wonder if **Samantha Wildwhiskers** sent this pigeon," I said.

"You mean that CAT who secretly reads your books?" asked my nephew.

I **NODDED**. "She sends carrier pigeons to get in touch with me."

Just as I was thinking about Samantha, my **SECRET** feline fan, two things happened.

(1) The pigeon dropped a rolled-up note on my desk, and (2) the pigeon dropped a **stink bomb** on my head!

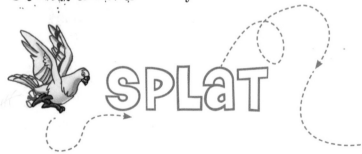

SPLAT

"Looks like our pigeon friend wants us to know that the message is for you!" Bugsy Wugsy said, giggling.

EEEEWWWW!

SPLAT

WHAT SHOULD
I WEAR?

After scrubbing my fur with **HOT** water and industrial-strength **CHEDDAR-SCENTED SOAP**, I returned to my office to read the note.

When I did, my fur stood on **end**.

Cheese niblets!

The message wasn't from Samantha. It was from **Kitty** and **SCOUT**, two of the children of the king of the pirate cats!

The note said that the cats were on their way to Mouse Island. They had set sail on their ship *The Black Hurricane* and were out to steal our beloved **Mousey Liberty**!

"The New Mouse City Statue of Liberty? But why would they want that?" Bugsy wondered aloud.

"I don't know," I murmured, my mind *whirling*.

A shipful of **CATS** headed for Mouse Island! What should I do? What should I say? What should I **WEAR**? After all, a suit and tie weren't exactly **fighting** clothes. Maybe I could find some boxing gloves. . . .

I was still thinking about **boxing gloves** when Benjamin piped up.

"I have an idea. What is the thing that cats fear the most?" he asked.

"Water?" I guessed.

"Attack dogs?" Bugsy suggested.

Benjamin shook his head again and again until finally Bugsy yelled, "We give up! What is it?"

Then Benjamin leaned in close to us and whispered his idea — which, I must say, was fabumouse! Did I mention that my nephew is not only sweet and generous, but is also super-smart?

ON *THE BLACK HURRICANE*

Meanwhile, *The Black Hurricane* crossed the dark **Catnip Ocean**, headed toward Mouse Island. Unfortunately for the cats, it wasn't all smooth sailing. In fact, as soon as they left Fort Feline, they met up with a furious storm. **GUSTS** of wind howled like Catardone's cousin Hairless when he once fell overboard. **Yikes!**

As the ship bobbed up and down, far below in the storeroom, two stowaways shivered. They were Kitty and Scout!

"My stomach!" meowed Scout, turning **green** from seasickness.

"Didn't I tell you it wasn't a good idea to eat that **TUNA SUB** before we boarded?"

Kitty scolded her brother.

"Did you have to mention **tuna**?" Scout wailed.

The kittens weren't the only ones **whining**. On deck, the crew had broken out into a noisy fight.

"Ouch, you stepped on my paw!" yelled a cat.

"Watch the tail!" **meowed** another.

"Don't make me claw you, Fish

Breath!" warned someone else.

It was an all-out BRAWL.

Before long, ear-piercing yowls joined the **rumbling** thunder and **crackling** lightning overhead.

If you ask me, those cats all needed some anger management sessions, or maybe just a relaxing yoga class to **de-stress**.

TEN GOLDEN SPEEDBOATS!

While the fighting **raged** above deck, Kitty and Scout waited for the storm to end. Suddenly, they heard a laugh coming from the staircase and the voice of a pirate cat DESCENDING into the storeroom.

It was Tersilla, along with the two new crew members, Thugsy and Killer.

"Quick, HIDE!" whispered Kitty.

The twins immediately climbed into two barrels filled with stinky food. The sign on one barrel read "**FREEZE-DRIED COD CAKES**: *Only the highest-quality fish!*"

The second barrel contained "**POWDERED MILK**: *Just add water and lap it up!*"

"Blech! I never want to eat another **cod**

cake as long as I live!" grumbled Scout.

"Better keep quiet," warned Kitty, "or you won't **live** long enough to eat anything. We can't let Tersilla discover us!"

Tersilla, Thugsy, and Killer reached the storeroom just as the kittens **pulled** the lids over their barrels.

"Your plan is purrfect!" exclaimed Thugsy.

"**SHHH!** We don't want to be heard!" responded Tersilla. "Now, let's review. I want to be sure that you understand the plan."

Thugsy and Killer looked at her **FEARFULLY**.

FREEZE-DRIED COD CAKES
ONLY THE HIGHEST-QUALITY FISH!

POWDERED MILK
JUST ADD WATER AND LAP IT UP!

"Umm, you start, Thugs, you are smarter than I am. . . ." Killer mumbled.

"Oh, no, go ahead, Kill, you're better at explaining things. . . ." Thugsy countered.

"MeoWWW! You hopeless strays!" Tersilla cried. "Must I repeat myself again? This time, listen carefully. My dad wants to drag the giant statue from Mouse Island all the way across the ocean back to Fort Feline. Even a kitten could see that it's an impossible feat! While my dear dad wastes his time bombing the whole statue, we will use a small blast of DYNAMITE to break off its lightest part. . . ."

"The piece of cheese!" Thugsy and Killer exclaimed in unison.

"Exactly! That piece alone is worth at least ten GOLDEN speedboats and will be transportable even with a tiny motorboat!" Tersilla finished.

Killer clapped his paws happily. "I get it! Now we just have to **SWIM** back to Cat Island, get a motorboat, drive it back to New Mouse City, and —" he babbled.

Tersilla cut him off with a **piercing** glare.

"Don't be a fool, Killer!" she **MEOWED**. "First, we're not going to swim back to Cat Island. We're cats! We hate **water**! We'll steal a motorboat at New Mouse City. Then Killer will climb up the statue to the piece of cheese and position the dynamite so that the cheese falls into the motorboat."

"Why do I have to go and not Thugsy?" Killer protested.

"Oh, don't be such a **kitten**,"

Thugsy shot back.

"I'm not a kitten, you're a kitten!" Killer whined.

"No, you are!"

"No, you are!"

"Quit the whining before I throw you two overboard!" Tersilla hissed, pulling the two cats apart. If she could just get these

two furbrains to cooperate, she could steal the GOLDEN cheese, and she'd be rich, rich, rich!

THUMP THUMP THUMP

After Tersilla and her two helpers left, Kitty **POPPED** up from the barrel she was hiding in. "Whew! That was a close call," she told Scout.

"You're telling me," said Scout. "It's a good thing Tersilla wasn't looking for a **SNACK**. You know how she loves these cod cakes."

"Only the highest-quality fish!" Kitty giggled. But before the two could **CLiMB** out of their hiding spots, they heard heavy pawsteps at the top of the **STAIRS**. As they listened, the pawsteps came closer and closer. . . .

THUMP

THUMP

THUMP

THUMP

THUMP

THUMP

It was **BONZO**, carrying some platters filled with smelly leftover fish.

"What is this place, Cat Central Terminal?" Scout grumbled as the twins hid again.

Bonzo arrived, mumbling to himself. "Meow! The boss sure can pack it in! I never saw a cat eat so much in all my nine lives! Now let's see what I can do with these leftovers. . . ."

Kitty and Scout held their breath as Bonzo stumbled around the storeroom looking for an empty container. At last, he found one.

"This will do," he said. "I can carry it up later when the boss wants his snack."

And so, without knowing it, he DUMPED

the leftovers right near Scout and Kitty's **HIDING SPOT**.

"This is purrfect, Scout!" said Kitty. "That container is **BIG** enough that we can both hide in it, under all those FiSH BoNeS. And you heard what Bonzo said — he's coming back later to bring it up

as a **snack** for Dad. He can carry us up to the deck without knowing! No one will see us."

"Good idea!" agreed Scout.

"Then we can **cut** the ropes that the cats are planning to use to tie the statue," Kitty continued.

Scout nodded. "There's only one **problem**."

"What's that?" asked Kitty.

"The **problem** is I don't know if I'm going to be able to survive more of this **stench**!"

LAAAAND HOOOO!

At dawn on the tenth day of the trip, the lookout cat yelled an announcement that woke everyone up: "LAAAAND HOOOO! Mouse Island port side*!"

Catardone stood on deck as *The Black Hurricane* entered the deserted port of New Mouse City.

Oscar Wildwhiskers was there, too. His royal cousin had insisted he write an **article** about their adventure to publish in the paper when the CATS returned to Fort Feline.

"I hope you're getting all of this down, Cuz," the king ordered. "I want a full-page spread in *The Cat Island Courier*. The headline could read something like 'Clever

---

* *Port side* means the left side of the boat toward the bow, the front of the boat.

King Makes Off with Mouse Gold!' Or just 'King Catardone III: Our Courageous Hero!' Or maybe . . ." he trailed off, deep in thought.

Oscar rolled his eyes. Ever since his cousin had been named king, he had fallen in love . . . with himself!

While the king continued rambling on and on, Kitty and Scout watched nervously from inside the container of stinky fish bones that Bonzo had brought up on deck. They had cut the ropes so that the statue couldn't be towed under the ocean. Now they scanned the port for any sign of Geronimo Stilton. Where was he? There wasn't a rodent in sight! Had the pigeon delivered the kittens' message?

"Tie up the statue! Prepare the cannons! Let's take this GOLD MINE down and bring it home!" shouted Catardone.

WHO CUT THE ROPES?

Bonzo interrupted the king. "Wait, **Your Felineness**! The ropes to tie up the statue have been **CUT** and can't be used!" he exclaimed.

"What?! **Cut?** Who would do such a thing?" meowed the king.

"I don't know, Your Felineness!" responded Bonzo.

"Of course you don't know! Why do I let you handle anything?! Where's Boots? Maybe he knows something for

a change. **BOOTS!** Boots! Where are youuuuu?!"
he **SHRIEKED** impatiently.

Where are youuuuu?! Boooots!

"Here I am, **YOUR CATSHIP**, at your service!" responded Boots, rushing up to his boss.

Catardone explained the rope situation to him, WAVING his paws about wildly. "Find me the traitor immediately! And find a way for us to take the statue!" he insisted.

Boots smiled. "PROBLEM SOLVED, Your Furryness! I thought some joker might try to stop us, so I brought extra rope," he said proudly.

"Did you just say you **thought**?

How dare you! I'm the only one who gets to **THINK** around here!" the king fumed.

Boots nodded and quickly wiped the smile off his face.

Catardone continued. "Of course I knew we brought extra rope! You don't have to tell me. I'm the one who thought of it. **Ha, Ha, Ha!**"

Then, turning to Oscar, he said, "Make

sure you're getting all this down, Cuz. I want this in my **BIOGRAPHY** someday. Everyone must know that I am a king who thinks ahead! I am **SMART**! I am courageous! I am . . ."

Twenty minutes later, Catardone was still **babbling** on and on about why he was such a brilliant king.

The twins listened to their dad with heavy hearts. "Now what are we going to do?" Kitty whined. "This **stinks** like rotten fish!"

They had only one other idea: begging. The two kittens leaped out of their hiding spot.

"Daddy, listen!" they meowed. "You can't **DRAG** the statue all the way back to Cat Island. You'll kill so many plants and animals in the sea!"

"**Aha!** I should have known you two had something to do with this!" Catardone said. "Don't be such **party poopers**! Now, step aside. Daddy has to give some important orders."

Then he yelled, "All paws on deck!"

PUFF!

The first light of DAWN was coming over the horizon, and New Mouse City was beginning to wake up. The pirate cats began to execute their plan to **STEAL** the statue.

Grappling hooks with rope attached were shot toward the statue. When it was finally **WRAPPED** in rope, Catardone ordered the cats to point the cannons at its pedestal. "Are you ready to knock it over? **FIRE!**" the king ordered.

A sailor lit the fuses, and everyone clapped their paws to their ears. But instead of the terrible **boom** they were expecting, the cannons made only a tiny **PUFF** sound.

"What is the meaning of this?!" Catardone roared.

"Your Felineness, someone is out to stop us. All of the cannonballs have DISAPPEARED!" declared the sailor.

STEAM shot out of Catardone's ears. His tail stood at attention.

"What happened to them?" he snarled.

"Someone must have thrown them in the sea," the sailor replied.

"But who?!" meowed Catardone.

Puff!

The cannonballs have disappeared!

Just then, the king turned to see Scout and Kitty trying to **SNEAK** away unnoticed.

"You two!" he **MEOWED**. "If I find out you two are behind the disappearing cannonballs, you'll get no more Kitty Krispy treats for the rest of the year!"

Oscar, who had helped the twins throw the ammunition into the sea, tried to help. "Don't be too hard on them. After all, they **meant well**," he reasoned.

"Meant well?!" roared Catardone. "Well, if they meant to drive their old dad purrfectly **MAD**, then they succeeded!"

Row!

Meanwhile, during the general confusion of **flying** grappling hooks and cannons that didn't fire, no one noticed that **TERSILLA**, **THUGSY**, and **KILLER** were missing.

Where did they go?

Taking advantage of all of the **chaos** on deck, they had lowered themselves down to the water aboard a life raft and started rowing away from the ship.

"Keep **ROWING**, cats! We need to move it if we want to beat my father to that statue!" Tersilla shouted as they headed toward the port of New Mouse City.

Thugsy and Killer rowed with all their **MIGHT**. As they neared the shore, they spotted a motorboat they could steal. When

they reached it, they were ready to grab the
GOLDEN CHEESE and race back to
Cat Island.

"We're going to be RICH, RICH,
RICH!" Tersilla predicted.

But she was wrong.

FLEA THEM!

As soon as Tersilla and her accomplices reached the docks of New Mouse City, a **surprise** was waiting for them. Within seconds they were attacked by an army of FLEAS!

My nephew **Benjamin** had figured out that the best way to keep the cats away was to hit them with their biggest **fear**: fleas!

Didn't I tell you he was smart?

Anyway, as the cats approached, the queen of the flea army called out, "FLEA THEM!"

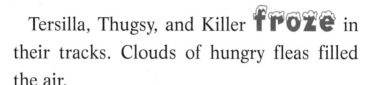

Tersilla, Thugsy, and Killer **froze** in their tracks. Clouds of hungry fleas filled the air.

"**MEOWWWWWW!**" the cats cried.

Thugsy and Killer grabbed the oars and began to row away as fast as their **paws** could move.

"Sour **salmon** sticks! They're right behind us!" Tersilla wailed.

From the deck of *The Black Hurricane*, Scout watched in shock as the life raft **SPED** back to the ship.

"What's going on?!" he shouted to Tersilla.

But it was so **noisy** on the ship, he couldn't hear her answer.

GET DOWN RIGHT NOW!

Catardone was yowling at the top of his lungs. "I want every whisker on deck! This is a **CATASTROPHIC** emergency! We need to knock down that monument, and we don't have one single **cannonball** to do it! I want everyone to think of a plan . . . now!" he ordered.

While the crew **frantically** tried to come up with an idea, Kitty **YANKED** on Catardone's sleeve. "Um, Dad," she said, "you might want to know that Tersilla took off with the life raft and . . ."

But the king wasn't listening.

"Is everyone thinking?" he roared. "I want to hear the wheels **TURNING** in your little brains!"

Then he turned to the scientists from the **CATLAB**.

"Come on! Where are all your brilliant ideas now?" the king demanded.

Just then, Bonzo coughed. Catardone **GLARED** at him, then turned back to the scientists.

"Well, I'm waiting for those ideas!" he meowed impatiently. "And if I don't get a good one, I've decided I'm going to knock down the statue with Bonzo's **HEAD**! It's probably the same size as a cannonball."

Bonzo gulped. Then he **CLIMBED** up the mast.

"Come down!" yelled the king. "I need your head!"

SORRY TO DISTURB YOU . . .

Right at that moment, a SMALL voice called out from the top of Mousey Liberty. "Um, sorry to disturb you . . ."

It was coming from a small balcony behind the crown on the statue.

It was me, *Geronimo Stilton*!

Um, sorry to disturb you . . .

After reading the note from the twins, Benjamin and Bugsy were up there with me, enjoying the view. We had finalized our plan of defense. Then we'd scurried over to the statue to get things started.

"Hey! It's Mr. Stilton!" Kitty cheered happily when she saw me. She and Scout secretly slapped paws in celebration.

Catardone was less thrilled. "It's that rat!" He SCOWLED. "What are you doing here? Who told you we were coming? Tell me who the traitor is! Wait till I get my paws on him!"

But I shook my head. There was no way I was going to rat out the twins.

"Sorry, but a true gentlemouse never reveals his sources," I answered, waving my paw. Then I grinned. "But since I heard that you were visiting our city, I wanted to give

you a *warm welcome* after such a long trip. So I took the liberty of asking some of your old friends to join me. . . ."

The king scratched his head. "Did he say *friends*?" he asked Boots. "Friends of ours in a city of mice? Who do you think he's *squeaking* about?"

Before the two pirates could figure it out, the entire army of FLEAS began heading toward *The Black Hurricane*. They zipped along the ropes that the cats had rigged up to pull down the monument.

In a flash, the cats realized they were in **danger**, and began racing around the ship's deck and yowling.

"Aaaaahhh! Fleeeaaaas!"

The only one who didn't **PANIC** was Oscar Wildwhiskers. He calmly took charge.

In a commanding voice, he yelled to the sailors,

"Cut the ropes, *quick*! Raise the anchor! Grab the oars! Let's save our fur!"

WE'RE DOOMED!

Too bad none of the sailors were listening to Oscar. Instead, they continued running around and around in circles, meowing at the top of their lungs.

"Help!"

"Here they come!"

"We're doomed!"

Just when it looked like the cats would be **scratching** for the rest of their lives, Scout had an idea.

"Hey, Kitty!" he exclaimed. "Remember the INVENTION that Dr. Redfur was talking about back on Cat Island? It was an anti-flea portable shower system!"

Kitty clapped her paws. "That's a great

idea, Scout! Let's find Dr. Redfur!"
she cried.

The twins took off in search of Dr. Redfur.
They found the scientist hiding belowdecks.

"Dr. Redfur! We've got to use your
anti-flea portable shower system.
It will help us chase the fleas away!" Kitty
said.

"But I don't know if it works," responded
Dr. Redfur worriedly.

"We don't have a choice! Come with us!"
Scout said.

As soon as they were all on deck, the king **STRODE** over with his paws on his hips.

"Listen up, Redfur. You better make this flea shower **thingamabob** work, or you'll be taking a permanent shower . . . in the sea!" he threatened.

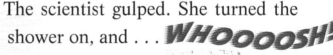

The scientist gulped. She turned the shower on, and . . . **WHOOOOSH!**

The disinfectant rained down all over the deck of the boat and made all the fleas cough and gag.

"Yuck! What a terrible **stench**! It's unbearable! Retreat!" yelled the queen of the fleas.

Quick as a pair of alley cats, the twins cut the ropes that linked the ship to our Mousey Liberty.

Then Oscar commanded the sailors to start rowing, and *The Black Hurricane* began to

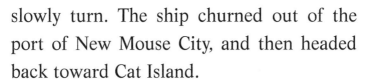
slowly turn. The ship churned out of the port of New Mouse City, and then headed back toward Cat Island.

As the cats were leaving, Catardone began to sob loudly. "WAAAAH! I almost had that GOLDEN statue in my hot, furry paws! What a waste! What a tragedy!"

I observed the scene from the top of the statue. I must say, it was pretty sad to see. The cats' tongues were hanging out as they rowed the **big** ship through the ocean. And the king was so **upset**, he looked like he'd need weeks to recover.

I felt so bad for the poor misguided cats, I picked up my megaphone and yelled, "It's not all that bad, King. Our statue isn't even made of GOLD. It's just YELLOW . . . like cheese, our favorite food!"

HOORAY FOR GERONIMO STILTON!

The next day, the citizens of New Mouse City organized a big PARTY in my honor to celebrate our triumph over the pirate cats.

"**Hooray** for Geronimo Stilton! **Hooray** for Mousey Liberty!" they cheered.

Then Benjamin pulled me aside.

"I was wondering, Uncle. Do you think Kitty and Scout will get in **trouble** with their dad if he finds out they were the ones who sent you that **WARNING**?" he asked.

"Don't worry, Benjamin," I said. "I think everything will be okay. Tomorrow, I'll write to Samantha Wildwhiskers, their cousin, to find out what happened."

I was pretty sure that once the cats made

it back home, they would be so relieved to have escaped the FLEAS that they wouldn't think about Mouse Island for a LONG while.

EVERYBODY PEDAL!

As *The Black Hurricane* neared the port of Fort Feline, the cats let out **sighs** of relief. They were glad to be home and to be totally FLEA-FREE!

WHEW!

Of course, there was one cat who was still complaining about the trip to Mouse Island, and that was King Catardone III.

Just to make himself feel better, he insisted that he'd known the **INSTANT** he spotted Mousey Liberty that it was not made of gold.

"I just knew it!" the king ranted.

No one believed this was true, but they didn't dare to contradict the king.

"We looked like **FOOLS** in front of those rats!" Catardone continued. "You want the electricity turned back **ON**? Forget it! Start **PEDALING** bicycle-powered generators. That's where you'll get electricity!"

Then Catardone tracked down Tersilla and her friends and demanded she explain why she ran off.

"Daddy, I didn't run off — I saw the FLEAS and was trying to help. . . ." she insisted.

The king rolled his eyes. "Nice try, but I'm not buying it!" he meowed. "As punishment, you will be in charge of cleaning up after the carrier pigeons!"

Nice try!

AMEOWZING, MY PAW!

When the ship pulled into the dock, Catardone was ready to head home. He needed a **LONG** catnap. Instead, he got **Hit** over the head with an umbrella!

"Son, I need electricity this instant! It's been weeks since Tabitha has been able to

Bonk!

use the fur dryer on me!" an elderly cat screeched.

It was the king's mother, and she was **FURIOUS**. Her fur looked like a bird's nest.

"But . . . your fur looks ameowzing. . . ." the king tried.

"AMEOWZING, my paw!" Catardone's mother raged. She pulled her son by the tail over to her bicycle-powered generator

Humph!

and forced him to **PEDAL** late into the night.

The Rodent's Gazette
Editorial Office

A SPECIAL DEDICATION

As for me, well, as soon as the party ended, I ran back to *The Rodent's Gazette*. Then I closed myself in my office to finish my new book. I called it *Shocking Ideas to Save Electricity!* And you want to know something? It was a big success!

Practical Advice to Save ENERGY

Sometimes, saving energy is just a matter of a few small tricks. Here's some advice!

- Take advantage of daylight as best you can.
- Always turn off lights you aren't using.
- Use energy-efficient lightbulbs.
- Dust your lamps periodically; a clean lamp gives off more light.
- Rediscover activities that don't use electricity, such as board games and outdoor games.
- Don't leave electronic devices (computers, televisions, DVD players, speakers, etc.) in standby mode. Turn them off.
- Keep doors and windows closed when heat or air-conditioning is on in your house.
- If it's cold outside, wear a sweatshirt or sweater indoors so you don't have to turn up the heat.
- If it's hot out, instead of turning on the air conditioner, draw the shades or close the blinds to help keep your house cooler.

My book was selling out like cheesecake ice cream on a **sizzling** summer day. And do you know why?

For three simple reasons:

(1) Because the **blackout** had had an effect on everyone in New Mouse City.

(2) Because it was full of **GOOD** advice on how to save electricity.

(3) Because inside the book there was an **embarrassing photo** of the illustrious king of the pirate cats being forced to pedal a bicycle-powered generator!

Do you know who sent me the **photo**? It was Scout and

Kitty. The very same **carrier pigeon** that they had used before came flitting once again through my office window. It dropped the message on my desk and once again . . . left a special little **surprise** on my head!

PLOP

UGH!

Before I looked at the message, I was ready to scream. But when I saw the photo of King Catardone, I laughed so hard I started **choking**. My secretary, Mousella, rushed in to see if I was okay. I showed her the picture, and she started laughing, too.

To thank the **carrier pigeon**, I

sent him back with some organic **birdseed** and some **gourmet** dried worms.

And to thank my feline friends, I included a special **dedication** in my book and sent them a photo of our staff. It read:

For Samantha, Scout, and Kitty —

Thanks for saving our precious Mousey Liberty!

Geronimo Stilton

Want to read my next adventure? I can't wait to tell you all about it!

FLIGHT OF THE RED BANDIT

One hot summer afternoon, I was trying to write, but I just couldn't get inspired. I needed a break! Who would've thought that soon I'd be in Arizona, hanging from cliffs and white-water rafting? Grandfather Shortpaws had sent me on a hunt for his old friend — the Red Bandit. What a fabumouse adventure!

Don't miss any of my other fabumouse adventures!

#1 Lost Treasure of the Emerald Eye

#2 The Curse of the Cheese Pyramid

#3 Cat and Mouse in a Haunted House

#4 I'm Too Fond of My Fur!

#5 Four Mice Deep in the Jungle

#6 Paws Off, Cheddarface!

#7 Red Pizzas for a Blue Count

#8 Attack of the Bandit Cats

#9 A Fabumouse Vacation for Geronimo

#10 All Because of a Cup of Coffee

#11 It's Halloween, You 'Fraidy Mouse!

#12 Merry Christmas, Geronimo!

#13 The Phantom of the Subway

#14 The Temple of the Ruby of Fire

#15 The Mona Mousa Code

#16 A Cheese-Colored Camper

#17 Watch Your Whiskers, Stilton!

#18 Shipwreck on the Pirate Islands

#19 My Name Is Stilton, Geronimo Stilton

#20 Surf's Up, Geronimo!

#21 The Wild, Wild West

#22 The Secret of Cacklefur Castle

A Christmas Tale

#23 Valentine's Day Disaster

#24 Field Trip to Niagara Falls

#25 The Search for Sunken Treasure

#26 The Mummy with No Name

#27 The Christmas Toy Factory

#28 Wedding Crasher

#29 Down and Out Down Under

#30 The Mouse Island Marathon

#31 The Mysterious Cheese Thief

Christmas Catastrophe

#32 Valley of the Giant Skeletons

#33 Geronimo and the Gold Medal Mystery

#34 Geronimo Stilton, Secret Agent

#35 A Very Merry Christmas

#36 Geronimo's Valentine

#37 The Race Across America

#38 A Fabumouse School Adventure

#39 Singing Sensation

#40 The Karate Mouse

#41 Mighty Mount Kilimanjaro

#42 The Peculiar Pumpkin Thief

#43 I'm Not a Supermouse!

#44 The Giant Diamond Robbery

#45 Save the White Whale!

#46 The Haunted Castle

#47 Run for the Hills, Geronimo!

#48 The Mystery in Venice

#49 The Way of the Samurai

#50 This Hotel Is Haunted

#51 The Enormouse Pearl Heist

#52 Mouse in Space!

#53 Rumble in the Jungle

#54 Get into Gear, Stilton!

#55 The Golden Statue Plot

#56 Flight of the Red Bandit

Check out these exciting Thea Sisters adventures!

Thea Stilton and the Dragon's Code

Thea Stilton and the Mountain of Fire

Thea Stilton and the Ghost of the Shipwre

Thea Stilton and the Secret City

Thea Stilton and the Mystery in Paris

Thea Stilton and the Cherry Blossom Adventure

Thea Stilton and the Star Castaways

Thea Stilton: Big Trou in the Big Apple

Thea Stilton and the Ice Treasure

Thea Stilton and the Secret of the Old Castle

Thea Stilton and the Blue Scarab Hunt

Thea Stilton and the Prince's Emerald

Thea Stilton and the Mys on the Orient Express

Thea Stilton and the Dancing Shadows

Thea Stilton and the Legend of the Fire Flowers

Thea Stilton and the Spanish Dance Mission

Thea Stilton and the Journey to the Lion's Den

THE KINGDOM OF FANTASY

THE QUEST FOR PARADISE:
THE RETURN TO THE KINGDOM OF FANTASY

THE AMAZING VOYAGE:
THE THIRD ADVENTURE IN THE KINGDOM OF FANTASY

THE DRAGON PROPHECY:
THE FOURTH ADVENTURE IN THE KINGDOM OF FANTASY

THE VOLCANO OF FIRE:
THE FIFTH ADVENTURE IN THE KINGDOM OF FANTASY

Check out these very special editions featuring me and the Thea Sisters!

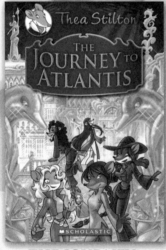

THE JOURNEY TO ATLANTIS

THE SECRET OF THE FAIRIES

He is a cavemouse—Geronimo Stilton's ancient ancestor! He runs the stone newspaper in the prehistoric village of Old Mouse City. From dealing with dinosaurs to dodging meteorites, his life in the Stone Age is full of adventure!

ABOUT THE AUTHOR

Born in New Mouse City, Mouse Island, **GERONIMO STILTON** is Rattus Emeritus of Mousomorphic Literature and of Neo-Ratonic Comparative Philosophy. For the past twenty years, he has been running *The Rodent's Gazette,* New Mouse City's most widely read daily newspaper.

Stilton was awarded the Ratitzer Prize for his scoops on *The Curse of the Cheese Pyramid* and *The Search for Sunken Treasure.* He has also received the Andersen 2000 Prize for Personality of the Year. One of his bestsellers won the 2002 eBook Award for world's best ratlings' electronic book. His works have been published all over the globe.

In his spare time, Mr. Stilton collects antique cheese rinds and plays golf. But what he most enjoys is telling stories to his nephew Benjamin.

1. Main entrance
2. Printing presses (where the books and newspaper are printed)
3. Accounts department
4. Editorial room (where the editors, illustrators, and designers work)
5. Geronimo Stilton's office
6. Helicopter landing pad

THE RODENT'S GAZETTE

Map of New Mouse City

1. Industrial Zone
2. Cheese Factories
3. Angorat International Airport
4. WRAT Radio and Television Station
5. Cheese Market
6. Fish Market
7. Town Hall
8. Snotnose Castle
9. The Seven Hills of Mouse Island
10. Mouse Central Station
11. Trade Center
12. Movie Theater
13. Gym
14. Catnegie Hall
15. Singing Stone Plaza
16. The Gouda Theater
17. Grand Hotel
18. Mouse General Hospital
19. Botanical Gardens
20. Cheap Junk for Less (Trap's store)
21. Aunt Sweetfur and Benjamin's House
22. Mouseum of Modern Art
23. University and Library
24. *The Daily Rat*
25. *The Rodent's Gazette*
26. Trap's House
27. Fashion District
28. The Mouse House Restaurant
29. Environmental Protection Center
30. Harbor Office
31. Mousidon Square Garden
32. Golf Course
33. Swimming Pool
34. Tennis Courts
35. Curlyfur Island Amousement Park
36. Geronimo's House
37. Historic District
38. Public Library
39. Shipyard
40. Thea's House
41. New Mouse Harbor
42. Luna Lighthouse
43. The Statue of Liberty
44. Hercule Poirat's Office
45. Petunia Pretty Paws's House
46. Grandfather William's House

Brigand's Isle

This way to the Rodent Straits

Tomcat Island

Pirate Ship of Cats

Hamster Islands

Blue Dolphin Bay

Cat's Claw Bay

Panther Archipelago

Coral Reefs

Swissville

This way to the Mousific Ocean

Stray Cat Harbor

Cheddarton

Mouseport

San Mouscisco

This way to the Ratlantic Ocean

New Mouse City

Mousefort Beach

N

W   E

S

Furflung Island

This way to the Sea of Mice

MOUSE ISLAND

Map of Mouse Island

Dear mouse friends,
Thanks for reading, and farewell
till the next book.
It'll be another whisker-licking-good
adventure, and that's a promise!

Geronimo Stilton